TODAY
I MADE
MY FIRST
RECONCILIATION

Written by
DIANNE AHERN

Illustrated by
KATHERINE LARSON

Published by Aunt Dee's Attic

Today I Made My First Reconciliation
Text © 2004 Dianne M. Ahern
Illustrations © 2004 Katherine Larson

A BOOK FROM AUNT DEE'S ATTIC

Published by *Aunt Dee's Attic*
415 Detroit Street, Suite 200
Ann Arbor, MI 48104

Printed and bound in Canada

Library of Congress Contorl Number: 2004102101

ISBN 0-9679437-3-6

1 2 3 4 5 6 7 8 9 10

First Edition

www.auntdeesattic.com

ACKNOWLEDGEMENTS

Dedication

This book is dedicated to the wonderful, giving, spiritual people who enrich my life every week: the Bible Study Group at St. Thomas the Apostle Church in Ann Arbor. Thank you. God bless you.

Acknowledgements

A very special thank you to all the people who helped make this book possible, especially. . .

. . . Father Eric Weber, Parochial Vicar of St. Thomas the Apostle Catholic Church, who provides a role model for all the St. Thomas family, but especially our children,

. . . Father Roger Prokop, Pastor of St. Thomas the Apostle Catholic Church, who continues to make me a better Catholic through his spiritual direction and gives us all encouragement to serve God and one another,

. . . Father Fortunato Turati, Servants of Charity, of the St. Louis Center, Chelsea, Michigan, who brings Jesus' love to life in his homilies—among the things he taught me is that 'God's love surrounds us like water surrounds a fish!',

. . . Josiah Shurtliff, graduate student of Theology at Providence College, friend, reviewer, and former assistant,

. . . Barbara M. Kelly, my best friend and sister, and her colleague, Erin Loos, for correcting my grammar and punctuation,

. . . all the others who preread and provided comments and advice on this book, including Kristin Bos, Leo DiGiulio, Christie McGuire, and Patricia Fulton,

. . . Ms. Fulton's third grade class at St. Thomas The Apostle Grade School (school year 2003/2004) and the Olszewski family for their presence and participation,

. . . Sacred Heart Parish in Campus, Illinois for allowing us to use images of their beautiful confessional.

What Does It Mean?

"Momma, what does 'reconciliation' mean?" asked Riley as he was sitting on the floor playing with his little sister Delaney.

"What do you mean, what does it mean?" said his mother, answering his question with a question. He didn't like it when she did that. It meant that sooner or later she would tell him to 'look it up in the dictionary.'

"Last Saturday, during our religion class, Ms. Kelly told us that we are going to make our First Reconciliation, and I don't know what that means," explained Riley.

"Oh," said his mother, distracted by a ringing telephone, "that means going to confession."

As he eavesdropped on his mother's conversation, he figured out that Maria was coming over to stay at his house for the afternoon. This was great. Maria lived next door and was his best friend in the entire world. They attended religion class together too. Maybe she knew what 'reconciliation' meant.

"Your friend Maria is going to be here in a few minutes," said Riley's mother. "Will the two of you look after Delaney while I fix a snack?"

"Sure, Mom," said Riley. He looked out the window and saw Maria running across the lawn from her house to his house.

Maria burst through the door and ran to give Mrs. Major a big hug. "Thanks for letting me stay with you," said Maria. Maria immediately sat down on the floor and began playing with Riley and Delaney. It was like she belonged to the family. Well, in fact, she did.

After their snacks, it was time for Delaney to take her nap. Mrs. Major gently picked up her daughter and, crooning a lullaby, took her off to her room. This left Maria and Riley alone. You could pretty much guarantee that when the two of them were left on their own they would find something to do, sometimes a good thing and sometimes a bad thing.

"Maria, remember how Ms. Kelly told us we were going to do reconciliation soon? Do you know what that means? I asked Momma and she said that 'reconciliation' means 'going to confession,' but I still don't understand," said Riley.

"Let's call Aunt Isabella," urged Maria. "She knows everything."

Maria picked up the telephone and dialed. She knew the number of her favorite aunt by heart. Maria could call her at any time.

Aunt Isabella told Maria that the Sacrament of Reconciliation was indeed sometimes called confession. She said that you tell God your sins in the

presence of a priest and then you recieve absolution.

Maria frowned as she hung up the phone. "It's worse than I thought. Aunt Isabella says you tell God your sins in the presence of a priest. But she didn't say why he needed to know them! Then the priest gives absolution, and that's what reconciliation is about. I still don't understand."

"Me neither," admitted Riley, shrugging his shoulders. "Come on, let's go outside and play soccer."

They played hard for a long time. Finally, Riley gave the ball a powerful kick. It skimmed across the grass, hit a light pole, and bounced toward Maria's house. Suddenly they heard the sound of glass breaking and shattering. Fear gripped the pair. This wasn't the first window they had broken. With eyes as wide as saucers, they looked at each other and then took off running for Riley's house.

Once inside, Maria said, "If I tell my parents we broke another window, they'll be really mad and will ground me forever."

"Let's not tell them," said Riley. "They aren't home, so they won't know we did it."

"Great idea. We'll pretend nothing happened," stated Maria. "Deal?"

"Deal!" said Riley.

Later that day, the children watched as Maria's parents returned home. After what seemed like hours, her dad came over to get her. "It seems there was an accident at our house while we were gone," he stated, looking at the children.

"Oh dear, what happened?" questioned Riley's mother. "Was anyone hurt?"

"No, nothing like that," said Maria's dad. "Somehow one of our windows was broken. I boarded it up for now, but we will need to get the glass repair people out first thing in the morning. Maria, do you know anything about a broken window?"

"No, I don't," said Maria. All of a sudden, she felt like her whole body was on fire. She glanced at Riley.

"Me neither," added Riley, looking back at her. Riley was sure that if he looked them in the eye either his mom or Maria's dad could tell he was lying.

The parents looked at each other with a shared suspicion that somehow these children were involved.

What is Sin?

"Remember last week, children, we learned about grace and that it is a gift from God that brings us closer to Him. Well, today we are going to learn about something that takes us away from God. That something is called sin," stated Ms. Kelly as she began the religion class. Ms. Kelly was the Director of Religious Education at their church and was in charge of getting the children prepared for the Sacrament of Penance and Reconciliation.

"Sin is something that we do that offends God. When we sin, we are actually rejecting God and His love for us. It is like saying 'God, You're not important to me.' That is a very bad thing to do.

"Think about it this way. God's love is everywhere. God's love surrounds us like water surrounds a fish. And, God's love fills us like water fills a sponge. When we do something that offends God, it's like taking away that water.

"What happens to a fish without water?" questioned Ms. Kelly.

"It flips and flops. It dies," replied the class.

"What happens to a sponge without water?" said Ms. Kelly.

"It dries out. It gets hard," replied the children.

"Correct," said Ms. Kelly. "Well, if we offend God by committing a very serious sin, it is as if we are telling God we don't need His water; we don't need His love. Like the fish that jumps out of the water, our souls die when we commit serious sin.

"If we commit a little sin, it is like taking a little water from the sponge. The sponge, and our souls, don't die, but they sure aren't healthy."

"Jesus gave us the Sacrament of Reconciliation to get rid of our sins. The Sacrament brings our souls back to life, just like the fish comes to life if it is put back in the water in time. This Sacrament also gives us the grace that we need to know, love, and serve God.

"Now, children, who can give me an example of a sin?" prompted Ms. Kelly. Lots of hands shot up and waived at her.

"You sin by disobeying or being mean to your parents," offered Danny. "Once I told my parents I hated them. I was being very bad. It made me feel awful."

"My mommy says it is a sin to say bad words," said Bridget. "Daddy said he will wash my mouth out with soap if I ever use a certain word again. Soap tastes really bad!"

"Taking candy from a store without paying is stealing, and I think that is a sin," said Matthew.

"Those are excellent examples of sins that offend God," said Ms. Kelly.

"Look in the back of your books, in the part that begins with *A Guide to the*

Sacrament of Penance and Reconciliation. Find the section called *The Commandments*," said Ms. Kelly as she had the children open their books.

"The *Ten Commandments* were given to us directly by God thousands of years ago, even before Jesus was born. Even though they are thousands of years old, they are still, and always will be, the rules that God gave us to live by. Besides the *Ten Commandments*, there are two *Great Commandments* that Jesus gave us through his disciples. The two greatest Commandments are to 'love God above all things' and to 'love your neighbor as yourself'.

"If we break one of the Commandments, we are breaking God's rule. When we break God's rule, we commit sin.

"Going back to the fish and the sponge examples, we know there are two kinds of sin," Ms. Kelly explained. "The very serious sin, the one where we reject God's love, like the fish jumping out of the water, is called mortal sin. We commit mortal sin when we absolutely, positively turn our backs on God, do something we know is seriously wrong, and break one of the Commandments. The awful part about mortal sin is that if we die without having our serious sins forgiven, our souls are separated from God's love for eternity. Our souls become like the fish that cannot jump back into the water. We call that going to hell.

"The less serious and less deadly sin, the one that's like the sponge that's lost water, is called venial sin. A venial sin occurs when we do something that offends God, but not as much as a mortal sin. Venial sins are bad, but do not completely shut us off from God's love like mortal sins.

"Let's use Danny's example to explain the two kinds of sin. When Danny told his parents he hated them, he disobeyed God's Commandment to *Honor your mother and father*. If he really, truly did hate them, it would mean that he was rejecting God and His Commandment, and that would be a mortal sin. However, if he was disrespectful because he didn't get his way or he was disappointed with their decision, that would be a venial sin.

"Our consciences let us know when we sin and how seriously our sins offend God. Your conscience is that quiet voice in your head that lets you know when you are about to do something wrong, are doing something wrong, or have done something wrong. It comes from your soul and guides your decisions or what is called your 'free will'."

Maria and Riley looked at each other. "Did we sin by not telling our parents we broke the window?" whispered Maria.

"I don't know," replied Riley in a hushed voice. "We didn't do it on purpose, so I don't think it is a sin. But I don't think we should have lied to our parents. Let's ask."

As Riley raised his hand, Maria tugged on his shirtsleeve. She didn't want

Ms. Kelly to know what they did. She felt ashamed.

"Ms. Kelly, how do we know if we committed a sin if our quiet voice isn't sure?" asked Riley.

"I was just getting to that part," said Ms. Kelly. "In the back of your books is a section called *Examination of Conscience*. There is a list of questions for each of the Commandments. These questions should help you to determine if you have committed a sin."

The class read through the *Ten Commandments* and studied the ways to examine their consciences.

Ms. Kelly let the children take a break to use the bathroom and get a drink of water. Maria and Riley stayed at their table and took turns reading the questions for *Examination of Conscience*.

"Maria, I think we are in big trouble. This says you should not lie to your parents," said Riley, pointing to the questions after the Commandment to *Honor your mother and father*.

Maria sat quietly and frowned. Her dark brown eyes seemed to grow darker.

When the class resumed, Maria had a question for Ms. Kelly. "I know how I can commit sin, but how do I get rid of it?"

Just as she asked the question, Father Hugo walked in on the class.

"Good morning, Ms. Kelly. Good morning, children." As all the children's heads turned toward Father Hugo, he added, "You are learning about sin, aren't you? Well, you get rid of sin through a sacrament that includes confession, penance, and absolution."

Hearing the word 'absolution' again, Maria and Riley glanced at each other. That was a word that Aunt Isabella had used when she explained reconciliation.

Father Hugo explained. "Jesus gave us a wonderful sacrament, one that you will soon be receiving. It is called the Sacrament of Penance and Reconciliation. It is the way to have your sins forgiven and share again in God's love. You see, Jesus spent his life on earth teaching the Apostles, disciples, and other people how to live their lives and what to do if they disobeyed God. Jesus carried the guilt of all our sins on His shoulders," said Father Hugo, pointing to the crucifix. "He even gave up His life for us so that we would believe, follow the Commandments, and be able to live with Him in heaven. That's how much He loves us."

The children looked confused, so Father Hugo turned the class back over to Ms. Kelly. Time was nearly up for today's class, so Ms. Kelly dismissed the children. After all, they had several more weeks to learn all about temptation, sin, repentance, forgiveness, and reconciliation.

Lead us not into Temptation

After class, most of the children got together at the big field next to the church and began playing soccer. The day was sunny and unseasonably warm. The children were ready to let off some steam following their morning class with Ms. Kelly and Father Hugo. Too many big words!

"Father Mike, come and play with us!" shouted Enrico when he spotted Father Mike walking beside the church and reading from his prayer book. Father Mike was the new parochial vicar, and the children knew he could always be coaxed into playing with them.

"Only if you get Sister Mary Rose to play too," teased Father Mike as he saw Sister Mary Rose, the music teacher, leaving the church with sheet music in her hand. "It will be the girls versus the boys. Mary Carol, why don't you go ask her?"

Sister Mary Rose sensed what Father Mike and the children were up to. When she saw Mary Carol running over to her, she couldn't help but smile. Sister not only loved being with children, she loved to play soccer. When she was in college, she played on the Championship Women's Soccer Team. That was many years ago, but she still loved the sport.

"If you insist," Sister said after just a little pleading by Mary Carol. "Let me go and change my shoes."

Within minutes, Sister came out wearing running shoes and carrying a big cooler of lemonade and a basket of apples.

They played for nearly an hour. The children were starting to tire, and so were the adults.

"Time out!" shouted Father Mike as he made a 'T' with his hands. "Let's have some of that lemonade Sister brought."

As the children gathered around Father Mike and Sister Mary Rose, Father asked "What did you study in class this morning?"

"They told us about sin and the *Commandments*. I think it's pretty grown-up stuff. My dad says kids don't commit sin," said Anthony, shrugging his shoulders.

"I'd have to disagree with your dad, Anthony. Children are capable of committing sin, same as adults," said Father Mike. "For instance, just a little while ago I saw T.J. push Romano out of the way to get to the ball. Now if T.J. pushed him because they both were going for the ball, that is all right. But if he pushed him because he was angry with him or to bully him, well that's a sin. You do not need to murder to sin against the Fifth Commandment of *Thou shalt not kill*. You sin against the Commandment when you act in anger, take revenge, or give a bad example by your action."

"If you tell a lie to hide an accident, is that a sin?" questioned Riley. He was really bothered now about the broken window.

"Yes, it is, Riley. Lies are always wrong. Most lies are probably venial sins, but big, intentional, mean lies can be mortal sins," said Father Mike.

Riley and Maria just looked at him. They didn't want to say anything more. And they did not want to look at each other.

"Have you heard the phrase 'hit and run?' Here's an example. A man is driving his car and he accidentally hits another car. The man knows he did something wrong, but rather than stop and admit it and offer to fix the damage, he drives away. By driving away he is committing a sin against the Seventh Commandment, *Thou shalt not steal*. He just destroyed someone else's property, and destroying another's property is like stealing. If the police catch

him and he lies to them, then he is sinning against the Eighth Commandment, *Thou shalt not bear false witness against your neighbor*, because he is lying to authorities."

"So why doesn't he just tell the truth?" asked Danny. "That would be a lot easier."

"I agree," continued Father Mike. "The man could have told the truth, but he chose not to."

"Did the devil make him do it?" asked Erin. "Whenever I get in trouble, my mom says the devil must have made me do it."

"That is part of it, Erin," said Father Mike. "It's all about being tempted and making choices.

Father Mike picked up an apple from the basket and explained. "You all know the story of Adam and Eve. God told them not to eat the fruit from that one tree in the Garden of Eden. The devil, in the form of a serpent, came along and said it's OK to go ahead and eat from that tree." Father Mike tossed the apple from one hand to another. "Right then, Adam and Eve had choices to make. To follow God's instruction – don't eat the fruit – or to follow the devil's tempting – eat the fruit. Using their own free will, Adam and Eve decided to follow the devil. They ate from the forbidden tree and were immediately separated from God. They were tempted, they chose wrong, and they paid pretty big consequences, didn't they?"

"Yes," agreed the class.

"They didn't listen to their consciences, did they Father Mike?" asked Nadine.

"No, Nadine, they didn't. And as a result, all humankind was penalized," said Father Mike. "But these apples are OK. Help yourselves." He began tossing the apples to the enthusiastic children.

After the group broke up, Maria and Riley began walking home. "Maria, I think we did something like 'hit and run' when we broke the window in your house and then didn't tell our parents. We ran away from the scene of the accident and that broke the Commandments about *not stealing* and *not telling the truth*. We also lied to our parents and that goes against the Commandment to *Honor your mother and father*. We really are in big trouble! Now what do we do?"

"I am not sure. I don't want our parents to be mad at us, and I sure do not want to be grounded again. Let's just think about it for a while." replied Maria.

The ill effects of Sin

"Mrs. Jensen, I don't feel good. My stomach hurts," said Maria. It was the Monday after the religion class on sin. It was also soon after Maria and Riley accidentally broke the window and then lied about it.

"Do you want me to call your parents and have them come to take you home?" asked Mrs. Jensen.

"No," exclaimed Maria. Suddenly she was fearful she would have to admit her wrongdoing to her mother. Her older brother Luca would still be in school, and their dad was at work. That would leave Maria and her mother alone in the house, and she was afraid her mother would ask about the window. "Can I just go lie down somewhere?"

"Sure. I believe Sister Mary Rose has a sofa in her office. Want to go and lie down there for a little while?" asked Mrs. Jensen.

This sounded like the best idea. Maria went down to Sister's office where Sister welcomed her and made her comfortable on the sofa. Maria wasn't the first student, and certainly would not be the last, to take advantage of Sister's hospitality. Usually, unless it was a real illness with a fever or vomiting, Sister Mary Rose was able to help a sick child get better.

Sister was sitting at her desk humming when Maria decided she felt like talking. "Sister, do you remember last Saturday, after we played soccer, how Father Mike told us about sin and temptation? Well, can sin make you sick?" questioned Maria.

"Yes, I believe it can. Sometimes, anyway," replied Sister Mary Rose. Now she had an idea as to what was causing Maria's stomachache. "You know that sin separates us from God's love. The bigger the separation, the worse we feel. Oh, for a while we may feel pretty smart, like we are fooling God. But then we begin to feel lost and lonely and can even develop aches and pains.

"Do you know the Bible story of the prodigal son?" asked Sister. "There were two brothers. One went to his father and asked for his inheritance so he could spend it now rather than waiting for his father to die. That son took all the money his father had to give him and went off to the big city where he spent the money on foolish and sinful things. He drank too much. He ate too much. He squandered his money on evil things. One day he woke up and was very sad, very alone, very broke, and very sick in his heart."

"Oh, dear," said Maria. "What happened to the son? Did he die and go to hell?"

"Not at all. He realized that he had been leading a sinful life, and he decided to repent. That means he decided to turn away from his sinful ways. He ran home to his father, apologized for what he had done, and asked him for forgiveness. The father welcomed him home with open arms, knowing that his son had learned his

lesson. As a matter of fact, the father never stopped loving his son, just like God never stops loving us. The prodigal son's father was always waiting to accept his son back and he waited day after day for his return. But the father knew it was up to the son to want to come home and be forgiven," explained Sister.

"Sin separates us from our Father in heaven. But no matter what, our Father loves us, just as the prodigal son's father loved him. And if we admit our sins, promise to try not to sin again, and ask God to forgive us, He will! God the Father always wants to restore His relationship with us.

"If you haven't studied it already, there is a prayer you will learn to help you get over sin. It is called the *Act of Contrition*. I know there are two versions of it in the back of your *First Reconciliation* book. I have a copy here. Let's read the first version," said Sister Mary Rose as she sat down next to Maria.

"It begins, *Oh my God, I am heartily sorry for having offended thee*. That means I am sorry from the bottom of my heart for sinning. Then it says, *I detest all my sins because I dread the loss of heaven and the pains of hell*. That says I know how terrible sin is and that I understand the consequences. It ends with, *I firmly resolve to confess my sins, do penance, and amend my life*. My goodness, that says I will go to the Sacrament of Penance and Reconciliation, do what I need to get right with God, and try not to sin anymore."

"I think I understand," said Maria, clutching her aching stomach.

"Here's a song I like to sing to get God to help me to turn away from sin," said Sister as she picked up her guitar.

"You! You commit sins too!" Maria gasped at the thought of Sister Mary Rose being a sinner.

"Yes, I do, Maria. After all, I am human. The devil tempts me too. Why, the devil even tempted Jesus. Once Jesus went to the desert and fasted for forty days. He was really hungry. The devil came along and asked Him to prove He was the Son of God by turning stones into bread. Jesus told the devil to get lost, that man does not live by bread alone, but by the word of God. Jesus set an example of

how we need to love, serve, and obey God. You can read about it in the Bible in *Matthew Chapter 4* and also in *Luke Chapter 4*."

Then Sister began to sing:

Lead me, guide me, along the way.
For if you lead me, I will not stray.
Lord let me walk each day with thee.
Lead me, oh Lord, lead me.

I am weak and I need thy strength and power
to help me over my weakest hour.
Help me through the darkness thy face to see,
Lead me, oh Lord, lead me.

"That's really pretty, Sister. I think I'm feeling a little better now," said Maria.

"Good!" said Sister Mary Rose. "Here's a song you might know. It's called *Amazing Grace*. Let's sing it together."

After they finished the song, Maria asked, "Sister, is the grace in *Amazing Grace* the same grace that Ms. Kelly taught us about?"

"Yes, it is, Maria. What did you learn about grace?" questioned Sister.

"That it is a gift from God. I need it to be good, stay good, and to get to heaven. I lose it by committing sins. We receive special grace though the sacraments. When I make my First Reconciliation and my First Communion, God will give me special graces that leave marks on my soul. Once I heard Father Mike talk about grace at Mass. He said that we shouldn't pray for God to solve our problems. We should pray that God gives us the grace we need to solve our problems," stated Maria.

"That is a wonderful explanation, Maria," said an impressed Sister Mary Rose.

Before Sister could say anything else, Maria got a startled look on her face. She jumped up and ran to the door. "I have to go pray for some grace right now, Sister. Thank you. I will see you later."

With that, Maria hurried out the door and ran to the small chapel near her classroom. She knelt down on the bench and looked at the crucifix above the small altar. She wasn't sure what to do or say, so she just whispered. "Dear Jesus, please give me some grace."

That evening, Riley stood at the door to his father's office and watched. His father sat motionless in his chair, with his head bowed, his eyes closed, and his hands crossed on his desk. He was barely breathing. The first time Riley saw his father like this, he got really scared. He thought his dad was dead. Since then he has learned that his dad was just taking a prayer break. After a little while, his dad sat up, made the *Sign of the Cross*, and smiled at Riley.

"Dad, how come you pray so much?" asked Riley.

His dad chuckled as he gave his son a hug. "Oh, lots of reasons, son. I pray to thank God for all He has given us. I pray to ask for the grace to get me through another day and to help me with my work. I pray for blessings for you, your mom, and your brothers and sisters. I pray for friends and family members who are having a hard time. And, I pray to ask God to forgive my sins."

"Sins!" Riley exclaimed, as he turned to look his dad in the face. "We are learning about sin in my religion class! The teacher says we are all going to do something called reconciliation pretty soon. I think I understand sin. Sin is when you do something that offends God. But what does reconciliation mean?"

"Well, if sin offends God, don't you suppose that reconciliation takes away the offense?" asked his dad.

"Kind of makes sense," said Riley, still not fully understanding. "Ms. Kelly says I have to tell God my sins in the presence of a priest - that's confession - and then I get reconciliation. Is that how it works?"

"That's most of it. But you're forgetting a couple of steps. First of all, you have to admit that you did something wrong. That's the confession of your sin. Then you have to be sorry that you did it, and you must want to change your ways. We call that repentance. The big step you left out is asking for forgiveness. If we injure another person, we should ask that person for forgiveness. But in the Sacrament of Penance and Reconciliation you for sure have to ask God for forgiveness. Then, you have to do penance – that's a special deed or act or set of prayers that you do to show God you really are sorry. You also do penance for the good of your soul – to overcome sin. Then, after all that, a priest absolves you and you have reconciliation with God."

"Sounds complicated," said Riley. "Who invented this Sacrament?"

"Why, God did! In the Bible you can find example after example of God

working to help humans to overcome sin and to be one with Him. I noticed some examples in the back of your book on *First Reconciliation*. Let's look at a few." Riley scrunched his way onto the chair with his dad. They took turns reading the *Scriptural References* in the back of Riley's book.

After a while Riley said, "Dad, if I did something bad and it hurt you or Mom, do you think you could forgive me?"

"Yes, Riley, I could. In fact, I would have to forgive you if I want to go to heaven. You know the prayer, the *Our Father*. Look, it's here in your book. In this prayer Jesus teaches us to ask God to *forgive our trespasses as we forgive those who trespass against us*. That means I have to learn to forgive you if God is going to forgive me," explained Riley's dad. They read the prayer together out loud.

Riley sat up straight as an arrow. "Dad, the *Our Father* also says, *lead us not into temptation, but deliver us from evil?*" Isn't that asking God to help us to be good and not be like Adam and Eve?"

"That's right, son. I think you are really beginning to understand the Sacrament of Penance and Reconciliation."

Riley scooted off the chair and hurried to the door. "See you later, Dad. I have to go work on some stuff!" he said in near panic as he left the room. Riley ran to his room and quietly read the words to the *Our Father* again. Then he knelt down beside his bed and said, "Please, God, help me to be good and do the right thing. Forgive me for lying. From now on keep me from evil and temptation." He squeezed his eyes real tight and said, "Amen."

The Room of Miracles

"Who wanted to know what's behind that door in the back of the church?" questioned Father Hugo, the pastor of their church. All the children raised their hands. "I think it was Andrew who first asked," recalled Father from their tour of the church several weeks ago when they began religion classes.

"Children, behind that door a miracle happens!" proclaimed Father Hugo. Their eyes widened! "Behind that door, Jesus forgives us for our sins and God gives us special grace to help us to resist evil and grow in virtue."

"Now come follow me, let us see what's in there."

Father Hugo led the children out of the pews and down the aisle to the back of the church. He opened the mysterious door and had the children squeeze into the little room. They could see that the room only contained three chairs, a kneeler, and a small table with a Bible, a candle, and box of tissues on it. A screen separated two of the chairs. There was a crucifix on the wall.

"This is the reconciliation room," he announced. "Some people call it a confessional. It is where the priest goes to 'put on Christ' and perform the Sacrament of Penance and Reconciliation."

"You see, as ordained priests, Father Mike and I and other priests represent Jesus in the reconciliation room. This is where we absolve people of their sins. Jesus passed down this responsibility to us through the Apostles. The Bible recounts how Jesus appeared to the Apostles after he rose from the dead and he gave the Apostles the right to forgive sins."

> . . . he breathed on them and said to them, "Receive the holy
> Spirit. Whose sins you forgive are forgiven them, and whose sins
> you retain are retained." John 20:22-23

"I know that in the last few classes Ms. Kelly instructed you in the process of going to confession. It is also described in the back of your *First Reconciliation* book. I just wanted to explain it to you again so you see how easy it is.

"This is where the priest sits to hear confessions," said Father, pointing to the chair hidden by the screen. "The person coming to reconciliation is called the penitent. The penitent can either sit on the chair opposite me so we can talk face to face, or can sit or kneel on the other side of the screen so I do not see who it is. I listen to the person's confession, and we may talk for a little while so that I understand. Often I give some advice on how to overcome sinful habits. Then I assign the person a penance. The penance may be a good deed, a reading from the Bible, prayers, or whatever I think will help the person redeem himself or herself with God. Then the person says the *Act of Contrition* and I give absolution. Simple as that!"

The children unstuck themselves from the small room and went to sit in the pews closest to the reconciliation room. Father left the door open so they could go take another look if they wanted. "Any questions?" asked Father Hugo.

"You mean I have to go in there by myself and tell you my sins?" gasped Andrew, stretching to look back into the room.

"That's sort of right. It is just you and me in there," said Father Hugo, pointing to the reconciliation room. "But, when I hear your confession, I am Jesus listening and talking to you. And after I give you absolution, neither you, nor I, nor Jesus has to think or talk about those sins ever again. That's pretty special, don't you think?"

"Yes," agreed Andrew.

"Why do I have to say my sins out loud? If God knows everything, he knows my sins and he knows I am sorry," reasoned Marisa.

"You are correct, Marisa, God knows everything we think and say and do. He even knows what we are about to do. However, God wants us to accept responsibility for and to be completely honest about the bad things we do. You know that by saying words out loud they become more real than if we keep them in our thoughts. By saying our sins out loud, we are more honest and show that we are ready to accept responsibility for our actions. Once we say it out loud, we can get over it!

"There are other benefits of confessing out loud. When you tell your sins to the priest, he can offer you advice on how to overcome sinful habits. Also, if you

are having trouble describing your sins, the priest will help you to come up with the right words."

"Will you tell anyone what I confess?" questioned a worried Giancarlo.

"Never!" exclaimed Father Hugo. "If I do, I am committing a very, very serious sin. As a priest, I promise God to never, ever repeat what I hear in the confessional. That is my job and my vow. Even if someone confesses murder, I cannot tell anyone, not even the police."

"Wow," exclaimed several children, followed by giggles and whispering.

"How come we have to make our First Reconciliation before our First Communion?" asked Ryan. "My sister did it the other way around and now she says she doesn't need to go to Reconciliation any more."

"There is a very important reason we do it this way. Pretty soon, you will be preparing for your First Communion. At your First Communion you will receive the Body and Blood of Jesus Christ in the Eucharist. Because Jesus is pure in the Eucharist, we want your souls to be pure, that is without sin and in a state of grace, before you receive Him. The only way to ensure pure souls is through the Sacrament of Reconciliation.

"As far as not needing to go to Reconciliation, Ryan's sister has been misled, and I will talk to her about it," said Father Hugo. "You need the grace you receive from the Sacrament of Penance and Reconciliation to grow strong in your faith. Whenever you've been bad and you are feeling guilty and sorry about what you have done, you know that you can go to Reconciliation. It is through this sacrament that you can free your soul of sin and receive the grace you need to lead good lives.

"Children, I want you to promise me that throughout your entire lives if you have committed serious sin, you will go to Reconciliation before going to Communion. Do you promise?"

"We promise!" shouted the class, much to the delight of Father Hugo.

"What if I don't confess all my sins?" asked Maria. The broken window and the consequences were now haunting her.

"If you forget to tell a sin, don't fret about it. If it is an honest mistake, you

can make a good *Act of Contrition* and then receive Holy Communion. However, you must confess that sin at your next Reconciliation. If you don't confess a sin on purpose, well, that is very bad. If you receive Holy Communion without confessing your mortal sins, then you are committing another big sin. Remember, the most important Commandment is to love God with all your heart. If you lie to God, you are sinning against this Commandment."

"I'm afraid," admitted Yasmine.

"Now why would you be afraid? Or embarrassed?" questioned Father Hugo. "Who loves you more than anyone, even more than your parents? Who is your best friend?"

"GOD!" "Jesus!" shouted the children.

"Right! God loves you, and all He wants is for you to love Him back. This is your way of showing God how much you do love Him. So what is there to be afraid of or embarrassed about? It is between you and your very best friend. You have to be able to talk to and be truthful to your very best friend," concluded Father Hugo.

Yasmine and several classmates nodded their heads in acceptance.

During the next two weeks, the class worked on memorizing the *Ten Commandments* and learning how to examine their consciences. They practiced going to confession and learned about penance and the grace they receive through the sacraments. They learned to pray the *Our Father* and recite the *Act of Contrition*. They learned that the *Act of Contrition* is said after they confess their sins to tell God how sorry they are that they disobeyed Him.

Road to Salvation

"Children, please sit here, be quiet, read your books, and stay out of trouble," said Maria's mom in a hushed voice. Riley and Maria plopped their books on a pew in the back of the church and sat down in a huff. They did not like being stuck in church on a Saturday afternoon. Besides, by now their consciences were really bothering them, and they were snarly.

Both moms were members of the Altar and Rosary Society. It was their turn to decorate the church for this weekend's Masses. That meant they had to make sure the florist delivered the flowers to the church on time and that the flowers were watered and nicely arranged. Maria and Riley were not old enough to be left home alone, but they certainly were old enough to sit quietly in church and wait until their mothers were finished with their work.

Ever since the broken window incident, Maria and Riley felt awkward together. They both wanted to talk about what they did, but they couldn't find the right time or words. Now they had their chance.

"Maria, I feel awful because we lied to our parents about the broken window. What should we do now?" questioned Riley.

"Me too. I even got sick in school; I am so worried. We need grace to help us through this, but God probably is mad at us for lying. Especially lying to our parents! He'll never give us grace," pleaded Maria.

"Yes, He will. My dad says God is always willing to forgive. We just have to be sorry for what we did, ask forgiveness, and do some penance. God will forgive us if we are truly sorry," said Riley.

"Boy, am I sorry!" said Maria. "Hey, there's the reconciliation room. Let's go in and pretend we are going to confession. We will have to tell God about this problem pretty soon anyway."

The two slipped out of the pew and into the reconciliation room. They took turns sitting in the penitents' chairs and deciding which way was best – screen or no screen. Then they took turns sitting in the priest's chair trying to figure out if he could really tell who was in the room with him. They were beginning to act silly when they felt the presence of Father Mike.

"What are the two of you doing in here?" Father Mike's voice boomed from the doorway.

"Humm, uhmm," was all that could come out of Maria's mouth.

"We are practicing!" said Riley, with a strong voice that hid his embarrassment and fear. "We make our First Reconciliation pretty soon."

"Well, that is wonderful," said Father Mike with a gentle smile. He wasn't mad at all. "Is there anything I can help you with?"

"Yes, Father. I'm worried. If I die with sin on my soul, will I go to hell?" asked Maria.

"Well, that depends," said Father Mike. "The Bible and Tradition tell us that if someone dies with a mortal sin on his or her soul, that person cannot enter heaven. So, most probably he or she would go to hell or somewhere away from God's love.

"Now if you die with only venial sins on your soul, you will not go to hell, but you probably aren't pure enough for heaven either. In that case, you will go through a cleansing stage before you can be in heaven. The term we use for that is time in purgatory. It is up to Jesus to decide where and how long that takes."

"My cousin isn't Catholic, and she said her dad told her there isn't any place called hell. How do we know what's right?" asked Riley.

"I would look to the Bible to settle the argument. After all, the Bible is the official Word of God. Look in the back of your *First Reconciliation* books under *Scriptural References*. From what the Bible says about hell, I assure you that is not the place I want to be!" exclaimed Father Mike.

"Me either!" chorused Maria and Riley.

Looking at the crucifix on the wall, Riley asked, "Father, how come we say Jesus died for our sins? He didn't even know us."

"Very good question," responded Father Mike. "You will learn a lot more about this when you study for your First Communion. Put simply, Jesus is God who became man and dwelt on earth. Jesus came to teach us that salvation, that is living forever in heaven with Him, is possible if we turn away from sins and dedicate our lives to loving and serving God and one another. God sacrificed

His only Son so that sins might be forgiven." Then Father Mike quoted from the Bible.

> *For God so loved the world that he gave his only Son, so that everyone who believes in him might not perish but might have eternal life. For God did not send his Son into the world to condemn the world, but that the world might be saved through him.* John 3:16-17

"You see, Jesus carried the weight of our sins on His cross. He suffered the guilt of our sins as He hung on the cross. Then He died, knowing He had shown us the way. He said, *'It is finished'* (John 19:30). And, by rising from the dead, He showed us there is a beautiful eternal life with Him in the next world. It's all part of the mystery of our faith."

The children were fascinated. They didn't exactly understand what Father Mike had just said. And the word 'mystery' confused them. It would just have to wait for another day. Their minds were full. But, they believed.

"I am sure anxious to make my First Reconciliation," said Maria with a sigh.

"Me too," said Riley. "I can't wait."

"That is wonderful children. I am very anxious for you to receive this sacrament also. I do believe you are nearly ready," answered Father Mike.

The three of them looked up and saw the two mothers standing at the door to the reconciliation room. "That was a beautiful explanation, Father Mike," said Riley's mother. "Thank you for taking the time to talk to our children."

"Yes, thank you, Father. We only heard a little bit of your discussion, but I even understand more myself now," said Maria's mother.

They all walked out of the church together. As they reached the center of the church they turned to bow to the altar then genuflected before the tabernacle. At the door, they stopped to dip their fingers in the holy water and to make the *Sign of the Cross.*

Discovering the Meaning

"**A**re you sure we are supposed to be in here?" whispered Maria, as she and Riley peeked into his dad's office.

"Don't worry. It is all right. My dad lets me look things up in his dictionary all the time," said Riley with a voice of authority. He pushed the door open and flipped on the light.

"But that's when he is here. He isn't here now! We are in enough trouble with the broken window and lying about it. Let's go," said Maria as she tugged on Riley's shirt. She could see the crucifix hanging on his dad's office wall and knew it was wrong for them to be doing something their parents forbid. She understood that Jesus died on that cross for their sins. She certainly did not want Him to suffer any more because of her.

"Oh, come on," said Riley. "Our parents won't be home for another hour. The babysitter is busy taking care of Delaney. Besides, my dad doesn't care. Just as long as we don't touch his computer and don't mess with his papers."

The big dictionary sat on the stand opposite his dad's desk. The book was so big that the two of them had to stand on their tiptoes to read it.

Riley pulled a piece of paper out of his pocket and looked at it. Then he opened the dictionary up to the 'R' section.

"Here it is" said Riley spelling it out. "R-E-C-O-N-C-I-L-E. We should have looked it up a long time ago. It means 'to restore to friendship, compatibility, or harmony'."

"Oh, that must mean that when we confess our sins, we do it so that we can become friends with God again," surmised Maria.

"Yes!" exclaimed Riley. "That is exactly what it means."

He looked for the next word he had written on the piece of paper. "Now lets look up P-E-N-A-N-C-E.

"Here, it says something like 'it's an act of devotion that a person performs to show true sorrow for sins'."

"Penance. That's what the priest tells you to do to show that you are sorry

for your sins and to be reconciled with God. To be friends with him again."

"Now lets look up 'absolution'," directed Maria. "That word really confuses me."

"Wow, listen to this!" said Riley. "A-B-S-O-L-U-T-I-O-N. It means 'setting free from guilt, sin, or penalty'. It also means the 'forgiveness for an offense'. Remember, Ms. Kelly said that after we confess our sins the priest gives us a penance; then after we say the *Act of Contrition*, the priest gives absolution. Absolution must blot out our sins."

"I get it now!" shouted Maria. "Father Hugo said that after we receive the Sacrament of Penance and Reconciliation, neither God, nor he, nor we have to ever remember or worry about our old sins ever again because they are forgiven."

"This has to be the coolest sacrament God ever invented," claimed Riley, as they closed the dictionary.

The two of them settled into the guest chairs in his dad's office. After a short period of silence, Riley asked, "Maria, you know that when we do our First Reconciliation we will have to confess about breaking the window and lying to our parents."

"Oh, yes," said Maria. "I have been worrying about it for weeks. It makes my stomach ache. I want to confess and have it over with. I am really and truly sorry."

"Let's first tell our parents about it," suggested Riley. "I think Jesus would be more willing to forgive us if we first admitted to our parents that we were bad and we ask their forgiveness."

"All right," said Maria. "I just know that I will be grounded forever. You wait and see."

"Then that will be our penance from our parents. I think it is only fair. Don't you?" asked Riley.

Before Maria could argue otherwise, they heard the sound of the garage door opening. Their parents were home.

"As soon as the babysitter leaves, we have to tell them," demanded Riley.

Maria's stomach was full of knots, but Riley was calm and cool. They stood before their parents and told them the whole story about accidentally breaking the window but then lying to cover it up. Riley offered to pay for it out of his allowance. Maria said it was OK to ground her for a month, or even longer if they thought it was necessary. All they wanted was to be forgiven, to pay the penalty, and not to ever worry about not honoring their parents again. They wanted their love. They wanted reconciliation!

"We love you so much and we are so proud of you for telling us the truth. That took great courage," said Riley's dad.

"Please, do not ever be afraid to tell the truth," said Maria's father. "No matter what happens, we will always love you with all our hearts."

Then, after talking together for a few minutes, the parents told Maria and Riley that, in addition to the suggested penalties, they would have to write a paper about why the Sacrament of Penance and Reconciliation is important to them.

Maria and Riley looked at each other and smiled. They were glad to get the penance. Writing about the Sacrament of Penance and Reconciliation was going to be easy for them. After all, they had just learned a great deal about temptation, sin, repentance, forgiveness, and reconciliation. They each sighed a big sigh of relief!

As they sheepishly looked to their parents, all their arms opened up for a great big hug.

"I feel like the prodigal son," exclaimed Riley.

"You mean, prodigal daughter," giggled Maria, as she enjoyed the smothering hugs and kisses of the great big family.

Just one thing remained, however. They still needed to go to God and ask forgiveness for breaking His commandments. Fortunately, the children were making their First Reconciliation the next weekend.

First Reconciliation Day

On the day they were to make their First Reconciliation, all the children and their parents and guardians went to the church. Both Father Hugo and Father Mike were there to hear the children's confessions. There was nervousness in the air.

Before they began their individual confessions, Father Mike read to them from the letters of St. Paul and the Gospel of John. Sister Mary Rose led them in singing parts of *Psalm 51*. It went like this:

Ref: Have mercy, Lord, cleanse me from all my sins

Have mercy on me, God, in your kindness.
In your compassion blot out my offense.
O wash me more and more from my
guilt and cleanse me from my sin. Ref.

Indeed you love truth in the heart;
then in the secret of my heart teach me wisdom.
O purify me, then I shall be clean;
O wash me, I shall be whiter than snow. Ref.

Father Hugo gave a brief homily and provided final instructions on how to go to confession. Father assured the children that if they forgot what to do when they got into the reconciliation room, they should not be afraid or feel ashamed. Jesus would be there to help them, and Jesus would not let them down.

They all recited the *Confiteor* together. It was written on a little program that Ms. Kelly had prepared for them.

One by one, the children entered the reconciliation room and followed the lessons learned in class. Most of the children chose to sit with the priest for their reconciliation. A few very shy ones preferred to stay behind the screen.

After hearing each confession, the priest gave counsel and a penance. Then, after the child recited an *Act of Contrition*, the priest extended his hands over his or her head and said the prayer of absolution:

God, the Father of mercies, through the death and the resurrection of His Son has reconciled the world to Himself and sent the Holy Spirit among us for the forgiveness of sins; through the ministry of the Church may God give you pardon and peace, and I absolve you from your sins in the name of the Father, and of the Son, and of the Holy Spirit.

It was such a special day. All the children were happy and each felt lightness in their hearts that they had never felt before. This was the second sacrament the children had received that showered them with God's grace. The first sacrament they all had already received was Baptism. Baptism brought them into the Church. Now this Sacrament made them true participants in their own salvation.

When Maria and Riley had each completed their reconciliation, they knelt beside each other. For the first time in a long time they felt completely comfortable together. They were at peace.

"Father Mike told me to always remember that 'God loves me'," whispered Maria.

"Wow, Father Hugo told me the same thing," said Riley. "And I do really and truly believe that now. Confession has restored our friendship with God. I can feel God's love around me, just like water around a fish!"

"Me too!" said a brand new Maria. "Let's go find our parents and tell them we love them."

When the last child was finished, all the children and their families, the priests, teachers, and Sister Mary Rose gathered in the Parish Hall. A special meal had been prepared so they could all celebrate this very special day. Before giving the blessing before meals, Father Hugo looked around at the radiant children and their families.

"Why are all of you so happy?!" asked Father Hugo.

The children cheered in response, "Because, *TODAY I MADE MY FIRST RECONCILIATION!*"

A GUIDE
TO THE
SACRAMENT
OF PENANCE AND
RECONCILIATION

The reconciliation room is also called a confessional and, in some churches, it may be called the reconciliation chapel.

The modern reconciliation room is a quiet room where a person, the penitent, can meet with the priest and receive the Sacrament of Penance and Reconciliation. The penitent may choose to sit beside the priest or behind a screen so the priest does not see the person's face. Either way is acceptable.

Some older churches may still use an old style confessional. The confessional usually has three sections. The priest sits in the center and is separated from the penitents by a screen on each side. The penitents' sections have heavy curtains or doors to provide privacy. The penitent kneels and talks to the priest through the screen.

Priests can confer the Sacrament of Penance and Reconciliation anywhere that provides a little privacy. It can happen outside, in a car, in a plane, or wherever a person feels most comfortable talking to Jesus.

The Ten Commandments

I am the LORD your God: you shall not have strange Gods before Me.

You shall not take the name of the LORD your God in vain.

Remember to keep holy the LORD's Day.

Honor your father and your mother.

You shall not kill.

You shall not commit adultery.

You shall not steal.

You shall not bear false witness against your neighbor.

You shall not covet your neighbor's wife.

You shall not covet your neighbor's goods.

The Greatest Commandments

When the Apostles asked Jesus what was the greatest commandment, He responded saying:

> *"You shall love the LORD, your God, with all your heart, with all your soul, and with all your mind. This is the greatest and the first commandment. The second is like it: You shall love your neighbor as yourself."* Matthew 22:37-39

Jesus is saying that loving and honoring God, as established in the first three commandments, are the most important things in our entire lives. The other seven commandments proclaim how we should love our neighbor, our fellow man, and ourselves.

EXAMINATION OF CONSCIENCE

Before going to confession and receiving the Sacrament of Penance and Reconciliation, each person must recall his/her sins and the way those sins have offended God. Here are some questions to ask ourselves:

Commandment	Questions for Examination of Conscience
I am the LORD your God: you shall not have strange Gods before Me.	Did I think my desires were more important than keeping a promise to God or to my neighbor? Did I worship a false god? Did I put undue importance on material things?
You shall not take the name of the LORD your God in vain.	Did I use swear words or vulgar language that would offend God? Did I use the name of God, Jesus, or the Holy Spirit with disrespect?
Remember to keep holy the LORD's Day.	Did I attend Mass every Sunday and Holy Day? (Note: After you make your First Communion, you are obligated to attend Mass on Sundays and Holy Days.) Did I avoid unnecessary work on Sunday and try to stay away from businesses that make other people work on Sunday? Did I misbehave or have improper dress or cause others to be distracted in church?
Honor your father and your mother.	Did I talk back to or disrespect my parents, teachers, or other family members? Did I lie to my parents, guardians, or grandparents? Did I make fun of my parents, grandparents, or old people? Did I do all my house chores?
You shall not kill.	Did I get very angry with someone? Did I lose my temper? Did I keep bad thoughts in my mind? Did I wish evil on anyone?

Commandment	Questions for Examination of Conscience
You shall not commit adultery.	Did I have impure thoughts about another person? Did I show disrespect to persons of the opposite sex? Did I look at immodest pictures, shows, or internet sites? Did I do anything impure either alone or with others? Did I keep bad thoughts in my mind?
You shall not steal.	Did I take money or items that did not belong to me? Did I cheat on my schoolwork? Did I waste the time, money, or possessions of another person? Did I eat or drink to excess, allowing myself to give way to gluttony? Did I waste my money on foolish or vain things? Did I damage and not fix something that belonged to someone else?
You shall not bear false witness against your neighbor.	Did I tell untruths about a friend, acquaintance, or family member? Did I fail to tell the truth about something that I had done? Did I tell secrets without just reason? Did I listen to unkind talk about others and do nothing about it? Did I fail to forgive those who offended me?
You shall not covet your neighbor's wife.	Did I have impure thoughts about someone else's family? Did I feel jealous about someone else's family?
You shall not covet your neighbor's goods.	Did I envy my neighbor's belongings, car, house, or family? Did I spend too much money unnecessarily due to a whim or vanity? Did I fail to share fairly with my brothers, sisters, friends, or neighbors?

Sign of the Cross

In the name of the Father, and of the Son, and
of the Holy Spirit. Amen
***

Our Father

Our Father, who art in heaven, hallowed be Thy
name; Thy kingdom come; Thy will be done on
earth as it is in heaven. Give us this day our
daily bread; and forgive us our trespasses as we
forgive those who trespass against us; and lead
us not into temptation, but deliver us from evil.
Amen.
***

Hail Mary

Hail Mary, full of grace! The Lord is with thee;
blessed art thou among women, and blessed is
the fruit of thy womb, Jesus.
Holy Mary, Mother of God, pray for us sinners,
now and at the hour of our death. Amen
***

Glory to the Father

Glory be to the Father, and to the Son, and to the
Holy Spirit. As it was in the beginning, is now,
and ever shall be, world without end. Amen.
***

Act of Contrition (Version 1)

O my God, I am heartily sorry for having
offended You, and I detest all my sins, because I
dread the loss of heaven and the pains of hell,
but most of all because they offend You, my
God, who are good and deserving of all my
love. I firmly resolve, with the help of Your
grace, to confess my sins, to do penance and to
amend my life. Amen.
***

Act of Contrition (Version 2)

My God, I am sorry for my sins with all my heart.
In choosing to do wrong and failing to do good,
I have sinned against You whom I should love
above all things. I firmly intend, with Your
help, to do penance, to sin no more, and to
avoid whatever leads me to sin. Amen.
***

Confiteor/I Confess

I confess to almighty God, and to you, my
brothers and sisters, that I have sinned through
my own fault in my thoughts and in my words,
in what I have done, and in what I have failed to
do; and I ask blessed Mary, ever virgin, all the
angels and saints, and you, my brothers and sisters, to pray for me to the Lord our God. Amen.
***

Jesus Prayer

Lord Jesus, Son of God, have mercy on me,
a sinner. Amen.
***

Prayer to St. Michael

St. Michael the Archangel, defend us in battle.
Be our protection against the wickedness and
snares of the devil. May God rebuke him, we
humbly pray, and do thou, O Prince of the heavenly host, by the power of God, cast into hell
Satan and all the evil spirits who prowl
throughout the world seeking the ruin of souls.
Amen.
***

Prayer to the Guardian Angel

Angel of God, my guardian dear, to whom
God's love commits me here; ever this day be
at my side, to light and guard, to rule and guide.
Amen.
***

On The Sacrament of Penance and Reconciliation

Some people might tell you that it isn't necessary to go to confession or to receive the Sacrament of Penance and Reconciliation. They are wrong. Here are some Bible passages that will help you to see how important this sacrament is to God. These passages also demonstrate how Jesus passed the sacrament on to His Apostles, who in turn passed it on to our priests.

The days are coming, says the LORD, when I will make a new covenant with the house of Israel and the house of Judah... I will place my law within them, and write it upon their hearts; I will be their God, and they shall be my people. No longer will they have need to teach their friends and kinsmen how to know the LORD. All, from least to greatest, shall know me, says the LORD, for I will forgive their evildoing and remember their sin no more. Jeremiah 31:31, 33-34

"And so I say to you, you are Peter, and upon this rock I will build my church, and the gates of the netherworld shall not prevail against it. I will give you the keys to the kingdom of heaven. Whatever you bind on earth shall be bound in heaven; and whatever you loose on earth shall be loosed in heaven." Matthew 16:18-19

He summoned the Twelve and began to send them out two by two and gave them authority over unclean spirits. Mark 6:7

Then he opened their minds to understand the scriptures. And he said to them, "Thus it is written that the Messiah would suffer and rise from the dead on the third day and that repentance, for the forgiveness of sins, would be preached in his name to all nations, beginning from Jerusalem." Luke 24: 45-47

[Jesus] said to them again, "Peace be with you. As the Father has sent me, so I send you." And when he had said this, he breathed on them and said to them, "Receive the holy Spirit. Whose sins you forgive are forgiven them, and whose sins you retain are retained." John 20: 21-23.

If we acknowledge our sins, he is faithful and just and will forgive our sins and cleanse us from every wrongdoing. 1 John 1:9

And all this is from God, who has reconciled us to himself through Christ and given us the ministry of reconciliation, namely, God was reconciling the world to himself in Christ, not counting their trespasses against them and entrusting to us the message of reconciliation. So we are ambassadors for Christ, as if God were appealing through us. We implore you on behalf of Christ, be reconciled to God. For our sake he made him to be sin who did not know sin, so that we might become the righteousness of God in him. 2 Corinthians 5:18-21

Psalms

The *Psalms* are part of the Old Testament and were written hundreds of years before Jesus was born. During biblical times, the *Psalms* were sung or chanted during Jewish worship services. Today they are used in Church liturgy.

When Jesus and the Apostles were little boys, they would have memorized the *Psalms* so they could take part in services and also to use them in their prayers.

Many *Psalms* were written to praise God, some were to give thanks to God, and others were meant to help people through difficult times. There are also *Penitential Psalms* written to help people show sorrow for sins, ask forgiveness, and celebrate reconciliation with God. Here are some examples. Notice that in *Psalm 32*, it warns not to be stubborn like mules!

PSALM 32 - Remission of Sin

I

Happy the sinner whose fault is removed,
whose sin is forgiven.
Happy those to whom the LORD imputes no guilt,
in whose spirit is no deceit.

II

As long as I kept silent, my bones wasted away;
I groaned all the day.
For day and night your hand was heavy upon me;
my strength withered as in dry summer heat.
Then I declared my sin to you;
my guilt I did not hide.
I said, "I confess my faults to the LORD,"
and you took away the guilt of my sin.
Thus should all your faithful pray
in time of distress.
Though flood waters threaten,
they will never reach them.
You are my shelter; from distress you keep me;
with safety you ring me round.

III

I will instruct you and show you the way you should walk,
give you counsel and watch over you.
Do not be senseless like horses or mules;
with bit and bridle their temper is curbed,
else they will not come to you.

IV

Many are the sorrows of the wicked,
but love surrounds those who trust in the LORD.
Be glad in the LORD and rejoice, you just;
exult, all you upright of heart.

Psalm 119 – Prayer to God, the Lawgiver (Verses 9-16)

How can the young walk without fault?
Only by keeping your words.
With all my heart I seek you;
do not let me stray from your commands.
In my heart I treasure your promise,
that I may not sin against you.
Blessed are you, O LORD;
teach me your laws.
With my lips I recite
all the edicts you have spoken.
I find joy in the way of your decrees
more than in all riches.
I will ponder your precepts
and consider your paths.
In your laws I take delight;
I will never forget your word.

SCRIPTURAL REFERENCES

On Keeping the Commandments

In addition to delivering the *Commandments* (see the earlier section on the *Commandments*), God emphasized how we should keep His *Commandments* in other Scripture passages.

And his commandment is this: we should believe in the name of his Son, Jesus Christ, and love one another just as he commanded us. Those who keep his commandments remain in him, and he in them, and the way we know that he remains in us is from the Spirit he gave us.
1 John 3:23-24

If anyone says, "I love God," but hates his brother, he is a liar; for whoever does not love a brother whom he has seen cannot love God whom he has not seen. This is the commandment we have from him: whoever loves God must also love his brother. 1 John 4:20-21

On Anger and the Fifth Commandment

"You have heard that it was said to your ancestors, 'You shall not kill; and whoever kills will be liable to judgment.' But I say to you, whoever is angry with his brother will be liable to judgment, and whoever says to his brother, 'Raqa,' will be answerable to the Sanhedrin, and whoever says, 'You fool,' will be liable to fiery Gehenna. Therefore, if you bring your gift to the altar, and there recall that your brother has anything against you, leave your gift there at the altar, go first and be reconciled with your brother, and then come and offer your gift. Matthew 5: 21-24

On Redemption and Forgiveness

These passages tell us how important it is to be sorry for our sins and to ask God's forgiveness.

If you, LORD, mark our sins,
LORD, who can stand?
But with you is forgiveness
and so you are revered. Psalm 130:3-4

Though I say to the wicked man that he shall surely die, if he turns away from his sin and does what is right and just, giving back pledges, restoring stolen goods, living by the statutes that bring life, and doing no wrong, he shall surely live, he shall not die. None of the sins he committed shall be held against him; he has done what is right and just, he shall surely live. Ezekiel 33:14-16

If you forgive others their transgressions, your heavenly Father will forgive you. But if you do not forgive others, neither will your Father forgive your transgressions. Matthew 6:14-15

. . . for this is my blood of the covenant, which will be shed on behalf of many for the forgiveness of sins. Matthew 26:28

He delivered us from the power of darkness and transferred us to the kingdom of his beloved Son, in whom we have redemption, the forgiveness of sins. Colossians 1:13-14

On Temptation

The devil lurks throughout the world trying to destroy souls by leading them into temptation and hoping they will give in to evil ways. The devil even tried to tempt Jesus. Here is one account of it.

The Temptation of Jesus

Then Jesus was led by the Spirit into the desert to be tempted by the devil. He fasted for forty days and forty nights, and afterwards he was hungry. The tempter approached and said to him, "If you are the Son of God, command that these stones become loaves of bread." He said in reply, "It is written:
'One does not live by bread alone,
but by every word that comes forth
from the mouth of God.'"
Then the devil took him to the holy city, and made him stand on the parapet of the temple, and said to him, "If you are the Son of God, throw yourself down. For it is written:
'He will command his angels concerning you'
and 'with their hands they will support you,
lest you dash your foot against a stone.'"
Jesus answered him, "Again it is written, 'You shall not put the LORD, your God, to the test.'" Then the devil took him up to a very high mountain, and showed him all the kingdoms of the world in their magnificence, and he said to him, "All these I shall give to you, if you will prostrate yourself and worship me." At this, Jesus said to him, "Get away, Satan! It is written:
'The LORD, your God, shall you worship
and him alone shall you serve.'"
Then the devil left him and, behold, angels came and ministered to him. Matthew 4:1-11

Temptation of Adam and Eve

Now the serpent was the most cunning of all the animals that the LORD God had made. The serpent asked the woman, "Did God really tell you not to eat from any of the trees in the garden?" The woman answered the serpent: "We may eat of the fruit of the trees in the garden; it is only about the fruit of the tree in the middle of the garden that God said, 'You shall not eat it or even touch it, lest you die.'" But the serpent said to the woman: "You certainly will not die! No, God knows well that the moment you eat of it your eyes will be opened and you will be like gods who know what is good and what is bad." The woman saw that the tree was good for food, pleasing to the eyes, and desirable for gaining wisdom. So she took some of its fruit and ate it; and she also gave some to her husband, who was with her, and he ate it. Then the eyes of both of them were opened, and they realized that they were naked; so they sewed fig leaves together and made loincloths for themselves. Genesis 3:1-7

Temptation of Human Beings

Blessed is the man who perseveres in temptation, for when he has been proved he will receive the crown of life that he promised to those who love him. No one experiencing temptation should say, "I am being tempted by God"; for God is not subject to temptation to evil, and he himself tempts no one. Rather, each person is tempted when he is lured and enticed by his own desire. Then desire conceives and brings forth sin, and when sin reaches maturity it gives birth to death. James 1:12-15

On the Devil

Today we call him the devil. However, throughout history this evil fallen angel has been given many names. In scripture some of the common names for the devil include satan, dragon, serpent, and evil one. Here are some examples of the devil in action.

Now the serpent was the most cunning of all the animals that the LORD God had made. The serpent asked the woman, "Did God really tell you not to eat from any of the trees in the garden?" Genesis 3:1

A satan rose up against Israel, and he enticed David into taking a census of Israel. 1 Chronicles 21:1

Those on the path are the ones who have heard, but the devil comes and takes away the word from their hearts that they may not believe and be saved. Luke 8:12

Put on the armor of God so that you may be able to stand firm against the tactics of the devil. For our struggle is not with flesh and blood but with the principalities, with the powers, with the world rulers of this present darkness, with the evil spirits in the heavens. Therefore, put on the armor of God, that you may be able to resist on the evil day and, having done everything, to hold your ground. Ephesians 6:11-14

Do not be afraid of anything that you are going to suffer. Indeed, the devil will throw some of you into prison, that you may be tested, and you will face an ordeal for ten days. Remain faithful until death, and I will give you the crown of life. Revelation 2:10

Then war broke out in heaven; Michael and his angels battled against the dragon. The dragon and its angels fought back, but they did not prevail and there was no longer any place for them in heaven. The huge dragon, the ancient serpent, who is called the Devil and Satan, who deceived the whole world, was thrown down to earth, and its angels were thrown down with it. Revelation 12:7-10

On Hell

God tells us through the Bible that hell is a real place. He also tells us hell is not a place where we want to go. Here are some ways that it is described.

They shall go out and see the corpses
of the men who rebelled against me;
Their worm shall not die,
nor their fire be extinguished;
and they shall be abhorrent to all mankind. Isaiah 66:24

The wicked shall be angry to see this;
they will gnash their teeth and waste away;
the desires of the wicked come to nothing. Psalm 112:10

Then he will say to those on his left, "Depart from me, you accursed, into the eternal fire
prepared for the devil and his angels." Matthew 25:41

And you will say, "We ate and drank in your company and you taught in our streets." Then he will say to you, "I do not know where [you] are from. Depart from me, all you evildoers!" And there will be wailing and grinding of teeth when you see Abraham, Isaac, and Jacob and all the prophets in the kingdom of God and you yourselves cast out. Luke 13:26-29

A third angel followed them and said in a loud voice, "Anyone who worships the beast or its image, or accepts its mark on forehead or hand, will also drink the wine of God's fury, poured full strength into the cup of his wrath, and will be tormented in burning sulfur before the holy angels and before the Lamb. The smoke of the fire that torments them will rise forever and ever, and there will be no relief day or night for those who worship the beast or its image or accept the mark of its name."
Revelation 14:9-12

The Devil who had led them astray was thrown into the pool of fire and sulfur, where the beast and the false prophet were. There they will be tormented day and night forever and ever. Revelation 20:10

On Heaven

Heaven IS. It IS a place that God created for us. It IS the place where God IS. It IS a place where Jesus ascended as the second person in the Trinity. It IS a place where pure souls go to live eternally with God, His angels, and His saints. We can find descriptions of Heaven in the Bible; here are a few.

He sits enthroned above the vault of the earth,
and its inhabitants are like grasshoppers;
He stretches out the heavens like a veil,
spreads them out like a tent to dwell in. Isaiah 40:22

The LORD is in his holy temple;
the LORD's throne is in heaven.
God's eyes keep careful watch;
they test all peoples.
The LORD is just and loves just deeds;
the upright shall see his face. Psalm 11: 4, 7

So then the LORD Jesus, after he spoke to them, was taken up into heaven
and took his seat at the right hand of God. Mark 16:19

Do not let your hearts be troubled.
You have faith in God; have faith also in me.
In my Father's house there are many dwelling places.
If there were not, would I have told you that I am going to prepare a place for you?
And if I go and prepare a place for you, I will come back again and take you to myself,
so that where I am you also may be. Where [I] am going you know the way. John 14:1-3

For the LORD himself, with a word of command, with the voice of an archangel
and with trumpet of God, will come down from heaven, and the dead in Christ will rise first.
Then we who are alive, who are left, will be caught up together with them in the clouds
to meet the LORD in the air. Thus we shall always be with the LORD.
I Thessalonians 4:16-17

On The Importance of Confession Before Communion

Therefore whoever eats the bread or drinks the cup of the LORD unworthily
will have to answer for the body and blood of the LORD.
A person should examine himself, and so eat the bread and drink the cup.
For anyone who eats and drinks without discerning the body, eats and drinks judgment on himself.
1 Corinthians 11:27-29

On The Importance of Confessing Out Loud

For one believes with the heart and so is justified,
and one confesses with the mouth and so is saved.
Romans 10:10

H o w T o G o T o C o n f e s s i o n

It is easy to go to confession. There is no need to be afraid, but if you are a little nervous, pray to Jesus and your Guardian Angel to help you. You can ask the priest in the confessional to help too, because remember that the priest is sitting in for Jesus in the reconciliation room / confessional.

1. Know all your sins before you go into the confessional or reconciliation room. Remember that you do not need to tell your sins to anyone but the priest.

2. Kneel respectfully and keep your hands and feet still. In some churches, the custom may be to sit or stand beside the priest as you go to confession. If you are not sure what to do, just ask.

3. Tell the priest your sins, first the mortal sins and then the venial sins, and tell how many times you committed each sin. Remember, the priest is Jesus now and you are talking to Jesus.

4. If there is something you do not know how to tell, say to the priest: "Father, please help me. I have something to say but do not know exactly how to say it."

5. After you finish telling all your sins, say: "These are all the sins I can remember, and I am truly sorry for my sins."

6. Listen carefully to what the priest has to say. He may ask you questions and you need to answer them completely and honestly.

7. The priest will give you penance. Remember it. Your penance may be prayers, a reading from the Bible, or a good work that you need to do. By doing penance, we show God how very sorry we are for having offended Him.

8. After receiving your penance, you say the *Act of Contrition*, slowly and sincerely.

9. The priest gives you absolution. This is Jesus forgiving your sins!

10. The priest will bless you. You make the *Sign of the Cross* at the same time. When finished, you can leave the confessional / reconciliation room.

11. If your penance is prayers or a Bible reading, it is best to do it right after you leave the confessional / reconciliation room and before you leave the church. If it is a good work to be done outside the church, you should do it as soon as possible.

MEMORIES
OF MY FIRST
RECONCILIATION

My name is:_____

Today is:_____

The church where I made my First Reconciliation is:_____

The priest who heard my First Reconciliation is:_____

This is what my family and I did to celebrate my First Reconciliation:

_____

_____

_____

_____

_____

_____

_____

_____

_____

_____

_____

_____

_____

_____

THESE ARE MY CLASSMATES

(Insert a picture or list their names)

MY FAVORITE BIBLE STORY
ABOUT FORGIVENESS

(Describe or draw a picture of your favorite Bible story)

MY THOUGHTS ON THE SACRAMENT OF PENANCE AND RECONCILIATION

Why Reconciliation Is Important to Me
(Write about it or draw a picture)

THE BEST THING ABOUT THE SACRAMENT OF PENANCE AND RECONCILIATION IS....

(Write about it or draw a picture)

If I were sin, I would taste like _____

If I were forgiveness, I would taste like _____

If I were love, I would taste like _____

I think evil is the color of _____

I think good is the color of _____

My favorite color is _____

I think the devil smells like _____

I think God smells like _____